DATE DUE

Bug Your Mom Day

David Kirk

GROSSET & DUNLAP/CALLAWAY

This book is based on the TV episode "Bug Your Mom Day" written by Steven Sullivan, from the animated TV series *Miss Spider's Sunny Patch Friends* on Nick Jr., a Nelvana Limited/Absolute Pictures Limited co-production in association with Callaway Arts & Entertainment, based on the Miss Spider books by David Kirk.

ISBN 0-448-44269-8   10 9 8 7 6 5 4 3 2 1

It was Bug Your Mom Day in Sunny Patch, a day when bugs show their moms how much they love them.

Miss Spider was taking her mom, Betty Beetle, to lunch at Le Beestro.

Holley decided to surprise her by tidying the house.

"**I**'m going to make Mom the best Bug Your Mom Day gift ever!" announced Dragon excitedly.

"*No!*" insisted Squirt. "Mine will be the best!"

"No, *mine!*" the other kids chimed in, one after the other.

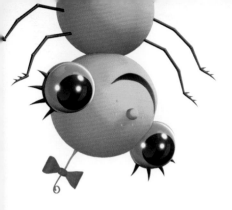

The only bug who didn't argue was Wiggle, who said simply, "I am going to make Mom a card."

The other kids giggled. A card? That wasn't nearly enough for the best mom in Sunny Patch!

The kids flew, hopped, and skittered out the door to look for the perfect gift for Miss Spider.

Pansy, Snowdrop, and Shimmer gathered big bunches of violets and forget-me-nots.

Dragon looked for the muddiest mud so that Miss Spider could have a mud bath.

Spinner collected beautiful seed pods. Squirt found Miss Spider a pea pod dish rack. Bounce went to the Dribbly Dell.

"Berry for Mommy!" he shouted, landing on his favorite bush. "Bigger!" he bellowed, bouncing to another, bigger berry.

Back home, the little bugs argued over whose gift was the best.

"Forget all that stuff! Look what I found!" yelled Dragon, bursting through the door with his tub of mucky mud.

Crash! The gifts were shattered! The house was splattered! Holley was not happy.

Neither were the little bugs—their gifts were ruined!

Wiggle offered his leaf. "My card is dry. We can say it's from all of us."

Nobody liked Wiggle's idea. His card was puny and plain. They knew they could do much better.

Spinner spun a new card. All the kids decorated it with violets, daisies, daffodils, dewdrops, and berries. When they were finished, Bounce came bouncing in rolling an *extra* fat, extra squishy jumbo blueberry! *"Bounce! No!"* everybuggy screamed.

It was too late. *Sploosh!* Sticky blueberry juice splashed everywhere.

Just then, Miss Spider came home.

"Oh my!" she exclaimed.

"We were trying to make you a super-spiderific Bug Your Mom Day gift," Squirt sighed.

Wiggle crept up shyly behind his mother.

"But here is a little card from all of us," he said.

"Why, Wiggle, this is beautiful!" beamed Miss Spider.

"But the very best Bug Your Mom Day gift of all is knowing how much my darlings love me."